Praise for Storyshares

"One of the brightest innovators and game-changers in the education industry."
— Forbes

"Your success in applying research-validated practices to promote literacy
serves as a valuable model for other organizations seeking to create
evidence-based literacy programs."   — Library of Congress

"We need powerful social and educational innovation, and Storyshares is
breaking new ground. The organization addresses critical problems facing
our students and teachers. I am excited about the strategies it brings to the
collective work of making sure every student has an equal chance in life."
— Teach For America

"It's the perfect idea. There's really nothing like this. I mean, wow, this will be a
wonderful experience for young people."   — Andrea Davis Pinkney,
Executive Director, Scholastic

"Reading for meaning opens opportunities for a lifetime of learning. Providing
emerging readers with engaging texts that are designed to offer both challeng-
es and support for each individual will improve their lives for years to come.
Storyshares is a wonderful start."
— David Rose, Co-founder of CAST & UDL

Across the Waters

Storyshares presents

Published by Storyshares, LLC
Inspiring reading with a new kind of book.

Storyshares
Storyshares, LLC
24 N. Bryn Mawr Avenue #340
Bryn Mawr, Pennsylvania 19010-3304
www.storyshares.org

Interest Level: Post-High School
Grade Level Equivalent: 2.9

ISBN 9798885977142
Book design by Saskia Globig

Across the Waters

Phoebe Angaye

Storyshares

CONTENTS

CHAPTER 1

"How could you bring an *akata* boy to this house, Chioma?"

Mom's words somehow draw out into a long hiss. Her volume, light as a feather, does not capture how her lungs rasp when she stresses on the word *akata*.

She no doubt wants to yell. The orange triangle print wrapper around her bulbous breasts can barely contain her.

Maybe bringing Darius to meet my parents wasn't the best idea.

You know when you're at that serious stage in your relationship? The weird "maybe we will get married or maybe we won't?" Yeah. Darius and I are at that stage.

And meeting the parents is one of the determining factors to decide if we *do* get married.

Standing in the kitchen trying to calm down my mom is not a good sign.

She has an iron lock hold on my wrist, chaining me to her. I shake my mother's grip around my wrist loose.

"He's a good guy. We've been dating since freshman year, Mom."

The words slip out. Her lip puckers in protest.

"*Mcheww*. Foolish girl. You should be bringing home an *Igbo* man! What have you been doing in college? Instead of getting good grades, you're busy dating!" she squawks.

Her satin black head cap falls back to expose dainty silver hairs.

"Stop it. I'm going back out there. You better respect Darius."

I don't give her room to reply as I make my way back to the dining room. I can hear my mom muttering, *"God, please, ooooo...."*

CHAPTER 2

Darius sits straight, looking forward.

My dad, on the other hand, inspects Darius like he's a foreign insect. When he cannot seem to find a fault, my dad zeroes in on Darius's piercings.

Darius's piercings gleam in the chandelier light like diamond polka-dots.

My dad hisses. Darius sits straighter.

I slide into the seat next to him and thread my fingers through his. Darius squeezes my hand. My dad's gaze shifts from Darius to me.

He looks as if he is trying to put the fear of God into me. My dad crosses his arms.

"Did you guys talk a little?" I ask.

My dad's frown somehow grows deeper. He simply sighs.

My mom comes back to the table, simply staring at the *egusi* soup she cooked. Steam no longer rises from it.

Darius clears his throat. "I was 'bout to tell Mr. Udo about how I decided to major in art."

Both of my parents gawk.

Slowly, my dad breaks into a slow clap. He shakes his head in wonder.

"Chioma. Chioma. Chioma! Which kind man have you brought to this house? Majoring in art? How will he support you and your children?"

While my father speaks, my mom nods at each word.

I resist the urge to roll my eyes. Of course, the man had to be the breadwinner. And of course, I had to have kids.

"Eheh! Tell this girl, ooo. She don dey craze," my mom says. She wipes the beads of tears forming at the crinkles of her eyes.

Darius looks to me for translation. I keep my eyes on both of my parents.

"I care about Darius. He means a lot to me. That's why I brought him here. I want him in my life," I say.

Darius nods in agreement.

"I love Chioma, Mr. and Mrs. Udo. I'm not perfect. Always tried, but couldn't be. But for Chioma?
I want to be as close to perfect as possible."

If I could kiss Darius right now, I would.

I'm not perfect. He's not perfect. But we're both
trying to make this work.

CHAPTER 3

My mom shakes her head. "Look. You don't even understand our culture."

Darius gestures to himself with his free hand.

"I'm willing to try, Ms. Udo. I'm notta 'bout to act like I know much about your tradition or customs. But I'll learn. I'm willing to learn."

I squeeze his hand in support. Our palms meld together with the rising intensity of the room.

My mom shakes her head and begins to speak in tongues.

My father? Well, he's gotten up as if he's been possessed by a spirit.

He paces back and forth in the cube-tight

space of our dining room. Finally, he stops, point-
ing a finger straight at Darius.

"What do you even do for work? What will
you do after you graduate?" His words come out
hurried and jammed.

This is ridiculous.

"Dad, we're still in college—"

Darius detangles his hand from mine and rises.
His expression is one of an archer aiming to hit
the bullseye.

He stands to meet my father.

CHAPTER 4

In Darius's eyes, a fire begins to burn. My mom watches, her mutterings in tongues coming to a halt.

"I work as a waiter at the moment. I won't lie. I'm not well off. I had to take out loans because otherwise, I can't afford to go to university.

"And if you're thinking I grew up in the 'hood, well, I did. I can't help that. This is who I am. I can't change any of those facts.

"I know I'm not what you expected. But the thing that matters is that I love Chioma. We haven't decided anything yet. But I want both of your blessings."

Darius stands tall, looking my dad straight in the eye.

My mother gapes.

Affection swells in my chest. He loves me. He said he loved me. We hadn't gotten to that stage, or rather that word, yet.

A vein on my father's forehead throbs. He gently rubs circles around the spot.

My mom rises, squeezing his shoulder.

"Get out of my house. You're not getting any kind of blessing from either of us. Chioma, you need to end this relationship."

Her words make this a shut and closed case.

But that's not how it's going to be.

I stand up and intertwine my hand with Darius. "No. I'm staying with him."

My mother promptly does the cross over her heart. The vein on my father's head pulsates again. He points at Darius and then the door.

"Leave. Now."

Darius kisses my cheek and lets my hand fall to the side. My heart stops for a moment.

"I'll let you guys sort yourselves out. Call me."

CHAPTER 5

My world reassembles. Thank God my parents weren't able to scare him off. He gives me one last look before leaving through the front door.

I face my parents. They still look like they want to hold a prayer session for me. Knowing them, they probably will hold a prayer session with or without me.

"Chioma. You cannot be with this boy. We will not accept him." Venom drips off my mother's every word.

I shake my head. "Can't you see that he makes me happy? Why can't you give him a chance?"

She shakes her head. "Chioma, you will come to see that some differences are just too great to overcome. We are trying to correct you."

"Differences. How are Darius and I so different? Because he talks a little different? Because I talk 'white?'"

My dad's anger dissipates like boiling water. Instead, a forlorn look takes over. He exhales as if the stress of the situation will follow.

"Listen to your mother. *Akata* boys? They will mess you up, Chioma. They deal all sorts of drugs and have baby mamas—"

Their words go in one ear and get jumbled in the middle.

Baby mamas? Drugs? Is that what they think of all African Americans?

Darius is nothing like that.

In fact, when we met, I was the one who was too drunk to walk home from a party. I went to the party without my friends, so I was alone.

CHAPTER 6

Darius had been driving drunk people back to their dorms. I ended up being one of those people. I gave him my number and told him to call me when I'm sober.

From there, it was history. If my parents knew how I met Darius, they'd ship me back to Nigeria in a Ghana Must Go bag.

If they only knew what a good guy Darius is. They wouldn't have treated him like that.

I throw my hands up in the air. "It doesn't matter if I'm African or if he's African American. We're both Black. At the end of the day, people will see us as Black. We're the same people."

My mother wags her finger at me like the African aunties who would chastise me back at home. "Chioma. We are not the same people. Americans may not see the difference, but there is a difference."

As if on cue, my dad starts wagging his finger at me too. At this point, they're looking like a pair of conductors.

"There are differences that are more than physical. There are differences that are cultural. African Americans were stolen from their native lands. They can never be the same. They've been cursed, Chioma," he says, and I try not to scream.

Cursed? African Americans didn't choose to be abducted. They did not choose to be traumatized. America doesn't see the nuances. It doesn't read the subtext. African Americans and Africans aren't that different. At the end of the day, when they look at our skin, they don't see the spectrum of all the colors "brown" can be.

To them, we're all "black."

I shake my head. "I'm going to my room. Goodnight."

Without another word, I rush upstairs to my bedroom, never looking back.

CHAPTER 7

"Don't worry. They'll come around," Darius says, squeezing my hand.

I sigh. If only he knew how stubborn Nigerian parents could be. Darius and I are a tangle of limbs as we sit on my bed. God forbid my parents catch us and figure out I've had premarital sex.

Or that he's here mere days after they threw him out.

Luckily, they're both at work and won't be back for a few hours.

"You don't know them like I know them," I mutter.

My finger is finding new interest in toying with the baby curls forming at his hairline.

He shakes his head. "Parents are always like that. S'not a big deal. Once they get to know me, they'll calm down."

I keep playing with his curls. A silent question comes to my mind. It's one which I dare not speak out loud.

What if they never come around?

I tuck the thought away.

They have to come around.

Darius makes me happy. I don't know what the future holds for us, but I don't want to lose him.

Am I ready to marry him? I don't know. I'm in university. I've barely experienced life and held down a real job.

But I do know this: I care about Darius.

Right now, I want to be with Darius. And I don't see that changing anytime soon.

CHAPTER 8

"So, why were your parents so offended by me doing art as my major?"

Darius's voice pulls me away from my thoughts. Uh-oh.

"Um. Well. They don't really believe in going to college to do 'easy' majors. Like majors that won't make you money."

My parents would have disowned me on the spot if I chose art as a major.

In an African family, you're either a doctor, lawyer, or engineer. Out of those three choices, I chose to be a doctor.

Pre-med isn't fun, but it gets my parents off my

back. My major also impresses the African aunties at family reunions sniffing for gossip.

Darius raises his eyebrows at me. "That's some bullshit. Art can make you money and it isn't easy."

Well, art is easier than pre-med, that's for sure.

I would kill to learn about art history rather than do another course in physics. Or biochem. Did I enjoy it? Not really.

But I'm looking forward to the end goal of helping people. And, most importantly, making my parents happy.

I purse my lips. "Well, art is a hard market to make money in. My parents aren't wrong about that."

He stares at me. Darius detangles his limbs from mine.

I hold him down. "Darius—"

"You think the same thing they do. Why are you so far up your parents' ass? You don't even want to be a doctor!"

CHAPTER 9

Now, I move away from him.

"You don't get it. I'm not up my parents' ass. My parents came to this country for a better life. I'm making them proud by choosing a profession that will make my family happy. That makes me happy. Wouldn't you want your parents to be proud of you?"

Darius scoffs at me. "I'm not my parents' puppet. In fact, I don't give a shit what they think."

Flames of anger light within me. "Then why are we meeting your parents on Friday? Why does it all matter, Darius?"

He gets up off the bed and begins to pull up his pants. I re-buckle my bra. We're both practically racing to get dressed. My pants are barely buttoned as Darius reaches for the door. I block him from exiting the door.

Darius glares at me. "Because it matters to you!"

I falter. Were we on the wrong page? He told me he wanted to meet my parents.

Did he feel like I was pressuring him?

"Darius—"

"Forget it. See you on Friday." Darius pushes past me, the door slamming behind him.

CHAPTER 10

I do go.

The paint on Darius's apartment curls back-ward, revealing another layer. Smoke spreads in the form of a thick wispy sheet from the apartment next door.

I scrunch my nose. It's weed. I'd know that smell anywhere. In the dorms, the musky scent was always accompanied by a masking flowery perfume.

Except for the occasional hearty laugh in the distance, you can hear a pin drop in the neighbor-hood.

Slowly, I knock on the door. There's movement

inside, and then the door opens. Darius stands there in a flat-ironed button-up shirt and blue jeans. He hadn't answered any of my texts or calls.

A mix of relief and, I dunno, happiness comes over me when he smiles at me. Despite everything, I want our relationship to work.

"My parents are at the dinner table."

I nod.

Darius takes my hand and guides me over to the kitchen.

It's not the first time I've been in Darius's apartment. I visited a few times before this.

Darius never really cleaned up before, but he did for today.

Where a mountain of clothes used to be, there is now a sofa. Maybe the sofa had always been there.

CHAPTER 11

Darius has laid out four plates. Potatoes with baked chicken and some vegetables.

Both of his parents look up when they hear us enter the kitchen. His mother looks just like the pictures Darius would show me.

Ms. Smith's bone-straight hair is something right out of a magazine. Her cherry-red lips stretch into a big smile once she sees me.

Ms. Smith reminds me of sweet, homemade apple pie.

Mr. Smith? A little of the opposite. While Darius has only pierced his ear, Mr. Smith has pierced both ears and underneath his lip. The black ink of a dragon peeks out from underneath his long-sleeved shirt.

Before we sit down, I place one bag in front of Ms. Smith and another in front of Mr. Smith.

I'd cooked some *egusi* soup for both of them.

Darius sends me a confused look.

"Oh! You brought us gifts? Thank you, um... how do you pronounce your name?" Ms. Smith's voice is like a dove singing on the arrival of a new morning.

I smile. It's not an uncommon occurrence. "Chioma. I'm Chioma Udo—"

"They know your name. I've told them about you," Darius cuts in, guiding me to my seat.

He sits next to me.

Mr. Smith eyes me like I'm a brand new species. "Your name sounds kinda foreign."

"Dad." Darius glares at his father, who returns the look.

I place a hand on Darius's arm. I smile. "It's okay. My parents are Nigerian. They wanted to give me a traditional name."

Mr. Smith's eyebrow goes up a notch. "Must have been hard transitioning to the United States."

Now Ms. Smith sends him a warning look.

Darius rolls his eyes. "She was born here, Dad."

"Sorry 'bout that."

It's all he says.

The silence is a twisting knife in the gut.

Mr. Smith just starts to dig into his food. Ms. Smith sends me a comforting smile before eating her food.

I reach over and squeeze Darius's hand. He smiles at me, but his smile doesn't reach his eyes.

CHAPTER 12

Darius starts digging into his food. I dig in as well.

A few minutes into eating, Ms. Smith clears her throat. She looks between Darius and me.

"I'm really glad to finally meet you. Darius tells me a lot about you," Ms. Smith says.

I smile.

"Thank you. I'm really glad I'm able to meet you. I hope I can get to know you better. I can always cook more soup for you as well. It's delicious, I can't wait for you to try it."

Mr. Smith lets out a rasping chuckle at that. Now it's my turn to raise my eyebrow.

Darius's fist is clenched into a tight ball. I'm beginning to see how Mr. and Ms. Smith divorced.

Darius rises from his seat. "What the hell is your problem?"

I rise, putting my hand on his shoulder. "It's okay, Darius. It's fine."

It's not okay, and it's not fine. But if I don't deescalate the situation, this may break out into a fight.

Ms. Smith glowers at Mr. Smith.

Mr. Smith turns from me to Darius. "Weren't you the one complaining to us how the soup tasted like crap and her parents are 'uneducated hicks?'"

Uneducated hicks? Our soup tasted like crap?

Was Darius looking down on my family the whole time? My stomach drops.

Darius lunges at him but I pull him back.

Ms. Smith ushers Mr. Smith out the door, slamming it behind them. I sink into my chair.

"Chioma—"

"Is it true? Is everything your dad said true?" I yell, and he shrinks back. He gulps.

"Yes, but..."

I slap his hand away from me when he tries to touch me.

I can't believe him. I can't believe this. I can hear Darius screaming my name, but I don't turn back.

When I walk out the door, he doesn't follow.

CHAPTER 13

He calls me out to a lake.

Darius kisses my face, my cheeks, my forehead. Everywhere but my lips.

He says we can start afresh and begin anew.

Darius says that it starts with this date. From now on, everything will change.

I simply nod.

Darius strips off his clothes and jumps into the lake.

The lake is as huge as a continent, and wide as an ocean. He gestures for me to get in, but I just stare.

Darius always forgot I couldn't swim.

Darius starts swimming away, becoming a small dot in the distance. Just like those before him, he reaches the other side.

It is then, I realize, we can never be.

About the Author

Phoebe Angaye is a contributing author to the Storyshares library

About the Publisher

Storyshares is a publisher focused on supporting the millions of teens and adults who struggle with reading by creating a new shelf in the library specifically for them. The ever-growing collection features content that is compelling and culturally relevant for teens and adults, yet still readable at a range of lower reading levels.

Storyshares generates content by engaging deeply with writers, bringing together a community to create this new kind of book. With more intriguing and approachable stories to choose from, the teens and adults who have fallen behind are improving their skills and beginning to discover the joy of reading.
For more information, visit storyshares.org.

Easy to Read. Hard to Put Down.

www.ingramcontent.com/pod-product-compliance
Lightning Source LLC
Chambersburg PA
CBHW071229170626
46809CB00005BA/1987